NO MORE SECRETS FOR ME

ORALEE WACHTER

No More Secrets For Me

Illustrated by Caroline Binch

Viking Kestrel

VIKING KESTREL
Penguin Books Ltd, Harmondsworth, Middlesex, England
Viking Penguin Inc., 40 West 23rd Street, New York, New York 10010, U.S.A.
Penguin Books Australia Ltd, Ringwood, Victoria, Australia
Penguin Books Canada Limited, 2801 John Street, Markham, Ontario, Canada L3R 1B4
Penguin Books (N.Z.) Ltd, 182–190 Wairau Road, Auckland 10, New Zealand

First published in the U.S.A. by Little Brown and Company (Inc.) 1983
First published in Great Britain by Viking Kestrel 1985

British Library Cataloguing in Publication Data

Wachter, Oralee
No more secrets for me.
I. Title
813'.54[F]   PS3573.A/

ISBN 0–670–80719–2

Printed in Great Britain
by Richard Clay (The Chaucer Press) Ltd,
Bungay, Suffolk

*An ounce of prevention
to Benjamin and his friends*

Contents

Foreword

Ever since I started dealing with readers' letters for a magazine, and then later a newspaper, problem page, I've known that sexual abuse of children is a commonplace event. I've known that a vast number of children are made uneasy at best, and deeply distressed at worst, by approaches from adults that they do not understand and can't cope with. And I know of the lifelong pain such an experience can cause.

Yet it is only in recent years that there has been any real public discussion of this all too common childhood experience or any provision at all made to help the children to whom it happens. I tried to write about it, I remember, back in the early seventies when I was first made aware of what was happening behind too many net curtains and closed front doors around Britain, but was blocked by well meaning editors who either didn't believe that the problem was as widespread as I told them I suspected it was, or didn't want to believe it. I have a particularly vivid memory of one 'macho' editor who went bright red and displayed bulging neck veins as he roared at me, 'That's disgusting! I won't have any such filth on the pages of my paper ...'

Now, fortunately, the subject is out in the open. With more and more newspaper reports of child abuse sometimes resulting in child death, we have been forced, as a nation, to look squarely at the fact that in this, one of the most civilized countries of the Western World, there are children whose lives are made a confusing hell because of adults who don't know how to handle their own sexual needs, and who turn to children for comfort and satisfaction instead of to their peers in age. We see more and more articles in papers and magazines and more and more books.

But we still don't see much aimed at the children themselves. It's natural enough that this should be so; talking to children about aberrrant adult sexuality feels in a way like imposing a form of sexual abuse on them. We – those of us who enjoy reasonable sexual health – want to rear children to be comfortable inside their own skins when they are adults. We want them to grow up self-accepting, happy to be what they are, able to enjoy their own bodies' feelings and reactions, able to share them with others' bodies. And telling children about the nasty ways in which sex can be used to hurt them doesn't feel at all like the right way to bring them to the sort of adult happiness we want for them.

But all the same they have to be told. It's no protection to wrap them in ignorance. They need to be warned, to be given permission to talk about disagreeable things if they happen to them, to be made to feel that they are not to blame if such things happen to them. A tall order – no wonder there has been so little information produced for children!

But happily, now there is. *No More Secrets for Me* is exactly what a great many parents and teachers have been looking for. It takes children by means of simple, direct and honest stories through the sort of problems that may arise. The first story, particularly, which deals with a child's natural modesty and which gives him permission to feel it and express it, is to be welcomed, and not just by children. There are a number of adults who need to be taught that children care about modesty, and need respect for it. And the other stories are important too, dealing with such everyday experiences as the adult who tries to get a child into a car, the young man who tries to share nakedness with a little boy, the step-father who uses his stepdaughter in a way that is wrong. Each and every one of these stories is going to be of enormous and lasting value to a great many children. I can't recommend it too highly.

Claire Rayner

Introduction

_____

It's not fair, but it happens. Someone you know, or someone you like, or someone in your family touches you, and you don't like it. It doesn't feel nice the way hugging and holding hands does. It isn't fun like wrestling with your friends is. It doesn't feel close and comfortable like it does when someone you love puts an arm around you.

If someone touches your body in a way you don't like, you may feel confused. You may feel as if you were tricked or forced into it. Or maybe the person makes you promise not to tell anyone and to keep the touching a secret. This book is about looking after yourself, just in case this ever happens to you or to a friend.

Talking Helps

Lee came home drenched from the rain. Josie, the baby-sitter, was there waiting for him. She came round every day to keep an eye on him until his mum got home from work.

'Hello, Lee,' she said. 'Take off your raincoat. You're dripping all over the place.'

He took his homework out of the pocket of his raincoat and looked at the watery purple ink. The wad of wet roneoed sheets was definitely too faded to read. No homework today, he thought.

'You're soaked,' Josie said. 'How about a bath to warm you up?'

Lee was surprised. Usually they had something to eat.

'A bath,' he protested. 'Why? I'm wet enough.'

Josie was already in the bathroom running the water. She pulled off his sweater and was about to pull down his trousers when the phone rang. Josie went to answer it.

'I can take my own clothes off,' Lee said to himself. He closed the door, got undressed, and slid down into the warm water. It felt nice. He knew Josie was talking to her boyfriend, Robert. They talked for a long time every day.

Josie put the phone down and called out. 'Lee. Pull the plug out before the water gets cold.'

A minute later she walked straight into the bathroom. She reached for a towel, wrapped him up, and started to rub him dry.

14

'Don't, Josie. I'll do it myself. Go and wait for me in the kitchen,' Lee said.

Josie looked at him for a minute and laughed. 'I expect you're embarrassed, Lee, aren't you? Just because you're naked. That's silly. I know all about boys. I've got two brothers, you know. They run around the house half undressed all the time. It doesn't matter at all.'

Without waiting for him to answer, she finished drying him all over. Even his bottom.

'It matters to *me*, Josie. I don't like it.'

When his mother got home he was still in a bad mood. 'I don't want Josie to baby-sit for me any more,' he announced.

'Why not?' asked his mother. 'I thought you liked her.'

Lee was confused. He didn't know what to say. Lee did like Josie, except for one thing. She always kept an eye on him, even when he didn't want her to. She never knocked on the door to the bathroom. She didn't let him get dressed by himself.

16

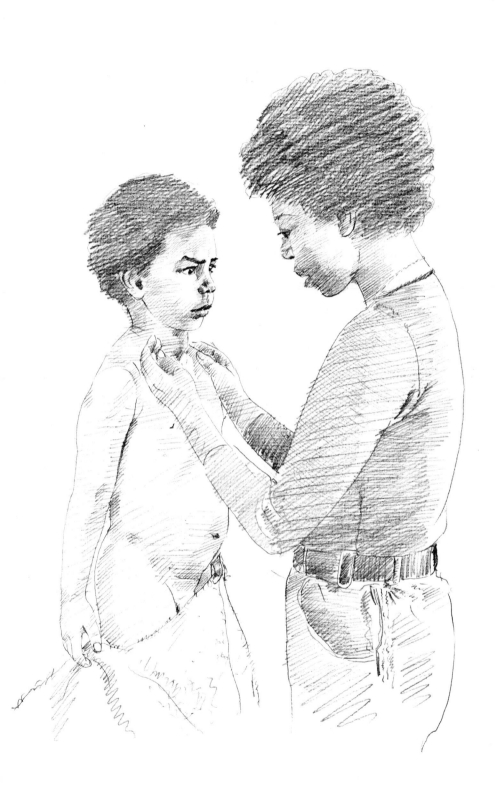

His mother put her arm around him and hugged him. 'Talk to me, Lee. If something's worrying you, I want to know what it is. Maybe I can help.'

'Well,' he began, 'I don't like Josie undressing me. I don't like her drying me, either. I don't want her to walk in all the time when I'm in the bath.'

'I can understand that,' answered his mother. 'Have you ever told her how you feel?'

'It doesn't do any good,' he said. 'She won't listen to me. She says I'm just being silly. Can't you get another baby-sitter?'

'Of course I can, Lee,' said his mother. 'If we can't get Josie to listen to you and respect your feelings, I will look for someone else. But first I'd like to talk to her and explain.'

'What will you say?' asked Lee.

'I'll say something like, "Lee and I want you to baby-sit. But only if you consider his feelings. That means listening to him and

respecting his privacy about his body." How does that sound?'

'Pretty silly. She won't listen.'

'We don't know that, Lee, until we try. I'll talk to her tonight.'

The next day when Lee came home from school, Josie was there, as usual, doing her homework in the kitchen. 'Got any homework today?' she asked.

'Yes. Spelling.'

'Let's make some French toast first. Then I'll test you. OK?'

'OK,' said Lee.

Josie cut some slices of bread. Lee broke an egg into a bowl and mixed it with a fork. Josie put some butter into the big black frying pan and lit the gas-ring.

'You know what?' said Josie.

'What?' answered Lee.

'Your mum and I had a talk. I suppose I didn't understand how you felt about some things.'

Lee slipped the first piece of bread into the

egg then laid it carefully in the hot butter. He felt funny talking about it.

'From now on I'll be more careful. I won't embarrass you any more. All right?'

'All right,' said Lee. 'Is it time to turn the toast?'

'Yes,' said Josie. 'Go ahead.'

'I always break it,' said Lee. 'You'd better help me.'

'Of course,' said Josie. 'That's what I'm here for. And speaking of help, let's get your spelling out, too.'

Friendly Persuasion

Lynn stood apart from the children at the bus stop. Every morning they pushed, and teased and jostled each other as they waited for the bus to creep through the rush-hour traffic. She stood in the doorway of a shop and read through her homework. Every now and then Lynn looked up to check the progress of the buses far down the road. That was when she noticed the battered old car. There was a pretty lady inside, talking to the children in the queue.

'Can anyone tell me where the library is?' she asked.

No one paid any attention to her. Some just shrugged their shoulders. Most of them went right on laughing and talking, as if she wasn't even there. The lady leaned right out of the window and asked again, louder this time.

'Can you please tell me how to get to the library?'

Lynn felt sorry for her. She knew the library was squeezed between two shops in the Centre. If you didn't know where it was, you would never find it. She stepped out of the doorway and went over to the car.

'The library is in the Centre,' Lynn said. 'Do you know where that is?'

'Yes, I think so,' said the lady, smiling at Lynn. 'By the Post Office isn't it?'

'That's right. Well, the library's there too,' Lynn continued, 'but it's very small. It's sort of hidden behind the chemist's. Right next to the supermarket.'

'No wonder I missed it then,' said the

woman. 'I must have walked right past it and didn't even see it.' The lady got out of the car and put her hand on Lynn's shoulder. 'Thank you so much. You're a very helpful girl. What's your name, dear?'

All three buses rolled up at once, and everyone piled on. 'Fares please. Hurry on now,' said the conductor.

Lynn saw the last few children get on the bus.

'Lynn,' she answered. 'I'd better go.'

Lynn turned and stepped on to the bus. She was the very last one.

'Mine's Mar . . . got,' the lady called, and she waved to Lynn as the bus pulled away.

After school, Lynn rode home on the bus with her best friend Ellie. They always went to Amir's sweetshop in the Centre and then walked home together. Today, when they got off the bus, Lynn noticed the same battered old car parked across the street. 'I suppose that lady, Margot, lives around here,' thought Lynn. Then she heard someone call her name. It was Margot calling her from across the street.

'Lynn. Lynn. Come over here. I want to show you something.'

'Who is that lady calling you?' said Ellie. 'Is she a friend of your mother's?'

'Not really,' answered Lynn, 'I just met her this morning at the bus stop. She says her name is Margot.'

'Margot? What did she want? Why were you talking to her? I mean, that seems a bit odd to me,' said Ellie.

'Oh, Ell! She just asked for some directions, that's all. There's no need to be rude, and anyway, she was very nice.' Ellie can be so unadventurous sometimes, thought Lynn.

'Well, what does she want this time?' said Ellie.

'Let's go and find out,' answered Lynn.

The girls crossed the street and as they got closer, they could see a tiny puppy snuggled up on Margot's shoulder.

27

'Oh, he's so sweet,' said Lynn, stroking the little round head and silky ears.

Even Ellie couldn't resist. 'What's his name?' she asked.

'His name's Mugs. Are you a friend of Lynn's?' asked the lady. 'What's your name?'

Ellie ignored the question and reached out to stroke Mugs.

'May I hold him?' she asked.

'Yes, of course,' answered Margot. 'Actually, I was just on my way to the library. Why don't we walk along together and maybe you can show me exactly where it is.'

'All right,' said Lynn, 'we're going that way anyway.'

The three of them walked to the Centre. Lynn and Ellie took turns holding Mugs while Margot talked on and on in a friendly way. She asked them about school and who was their favourite teacher. She wanted to know what sports they liked playing. Margot behaved as if she had known them for a long

time. She explained that she and her husband were new to this part of London, and she thanked Lynn and Ellie for showing her where everything was.

'Here's our favourite place,' Lynn said, when they got to Mr and Mrs Amir's sweetshop. 'My friend Adana works here in her parents' shop after school. She's so lucky.'

Margot smiled. 'I know what we'll do,' she said. 'I have to get some food for Mugs in the supermarket. Will you mind him for me? Then, I'll buy you both some sweets. How does that sound?'

'No thanks,' said Ellie. 'I have to go straight home after school. My Mum expects me.'

Margot looked disappointed. 'Oh, dear. That's a pity,' she said. 'It will only take me a minute. How about you, Lynn? I know your mum wouldn't mind.'

'Oh. Do you know Lynn's mother?' asked Ellie.

'Not really. But I'm sure she would understand,' answered Margot.

'Well, anyway, I have to get home,' said Ellie. 'It's a rule. Are you coming, Lynn?'

Before Lynn could answer, Margot held Mugs out to Lynn, dangling him in space. His little puppy feet pawed the air as Lynn reached for him.

'Thanks, you're a darling,' said Margot moving briskly away toward the store. 'I'll be back in a minute,' she called.

'I don't know why you're so nice to her,' said Ellie. 'You don't even know her.'

'You always think the worst of people,' said Lynn. 'I don't see what's wrong with minding her dog for a moment.'

'I don't think the worst. I just think it's odd, that's all. I mean, why is she so friendly and why does she want to buy us sweets? You can stay if you want, but I don't think I like her. I'll see you tomorrow,' said Ellie.

Mugs licked Lynn's neck happily, nibbled her fingers and then abruptly fell asleep in her lap. Soon ten minutes had gone by and Lynn began to wonder what was taking Margot so long.

'It's getting late, Mugs. I'm supposed to be home and here I am stuck with you,' she said to the puppy, who just went on sleeping.

Just then, the same battered old car drove up but this time there was a man inside. He opened the car door and walked over to her.

'Hello, you're Lynn, aren't you?' he asked. 'My wife forgot all about you and Mugs here. She sent me round to drive you home, before your mother starts getting worried about you. The car's just over there,' he said.

Lynn didn't know what to do. Maybe Ellie was right. Suddenly it did seem a bit odd. She knew better than to get in a car with a stranger but then again, Margot didn't seem like a stranger at all. And, this man was her husband, and he seemed to know who she was. She felt very confused.

The man put his hand on her shoulder and said, 'Look, I'm sorry about this. Some-

times Margot forgets things,' he explained. 'Not to worry. You and Mugs just hop in the car, and I'll have you home in a jiffy.'

'No, thank you,' said Lynn twisting out of his reach. 'I'd rather walk home. Here, you'd better take the puppy.'

'Nonsense,' he said with a friendly smile. 'Margot would never forgive me.' He reached out to Lynn, as if to pull her into the car.

Lynn jumped back out of his reach. She was still holding Mugs.

'No!' she said loudly, 'I don't want to.' She turned around quickly and ran as fast as she could to the safety of the sweetshop. She blurted out the story of Margot and Mugs to Mr Amir. 'There's a man out there,' she said, out of breath, 'he wants to take me home. I don't want to go with him. But, I have his dog and . . . I don't know what to do.'

Mr Amir listened. 'You stay here and play with Adana,' he said, 'while I phone your mother. She'll know what to do.'

When Lynn's mother arrived she was very

upset. She was also very glad to find Lynn safe. She hugged her and scolded her all at once. When Lynn told her what had happened, her mother became very serious.

'Lynn,' she said. 'Haven't I told you not to talk to strangers?'

'Yes, I know,' answered Lynn. 'But, Margot wasn't a stranger, not really.'

'A stranger is anyone your mother doesn't know, and I've never met this woman before,' said her mum.

'But she seemed so nice,' argued Lynn, 'and she remembered my name. I was just trying to be helpful.'

'Maybe she was nice,' said her mother. 'And maybe she wasn't. It's hard to know for sure. Nice people don't ask children to mind their dogs, or to go to places with them, or to do anything without their mum's permission. Nice people know that children are taught to be careful about things like that. That's why it's best to be extra careful. Running away was the right thing to do.'

35

'What about Mugs?' asked Lynn. 'What's going to happen to him?'

'Let's take Mugs along to the police station. I want to tell them what happened to you in case these people have bothered other children before. Maybe the police will recognize the car. We can report Mugs as a lost dog and if Margot doesn't claim him, I suppose we'll just have to take him home.'

Lynn cuddled Mugs. She wondered what Ellie would say when she heard what had happened. She could just imagine Ellie saying, 'See, I told you so.' 'Maybe Ellie is right,' thought Lynn. 'She doesn't take *any* chances.'

What If . . .

Sam had never been on a school trip before, staying away from home for a few nights. But here he was, in the country for one week. As well as the teachers there were two students who came along to help. One of the students, Mike, said that Sam's class was certain to win the Good Sportsmanship Award, provided they were all good sports.

Sam liked both the students. Mike built a huge campfire every night and got it blazing with only one match. Sam's friends called him 'Matchless'. The other student was Peter.

He could swerve a football on target from thirty yards out all day long. He was good fun.

But there were a couple of things about the school trip that Sam didn't like. For one thing, he wasn't used to eating with so many people at the table, passing bowls of cornflakes and grabbing at pieces of toast. And he didn't like getting undressed in front of everybody or taking showers with other people, either. He hated lending his soap and towel to Barry, who could never find his own things. But he did it to be a 'good sport'.

Every afternoon Sam's class went swimming. On Tuesday, Sam got ready to go swimming, but when everyone went to the swimming pool with Peter, he stayed behind. He wanted some peace and quiet. He flopped down on his camp-bed. It felt good to be alone, in the cool, dark tent.

'Hello, Sam. Are you in there?' It was Mike, peering in and squinting into the darkness. 'What're you doing? Why aren't you at the swimming pool?'

'Can't I skip it today, Mike? I don't feel like swimming,' answered Sam.

'What's wrong? Are you homesick or something?' Mike asked.

'A little bit,' Sam answered.

'I know what it's like. Sometimes I get homesick too, away all summer,' said Mike.

'You do?'

'Of course. I miss good home cooking and watching the telly. And Teddy.'

'Who's Teddy?' asked Sam.

'Teddy's my dog,' answered Mike. 'He's my pal. He's good fun. He'd love running around up here.'

'Why didn't you bring him with you?'

'We're not supposed to on a school trip; it's against the rules. *No dogs allowed.*' Mike sat down on the bed next to Sam and said, 'And you're not supposed to be in here, either. You know that, don't you, Sam?'

'I suppose so.'

'You could get into trouble if I told anyone. You know that, don't you?'

42

Sam nodded.

'But I know how you feel. Don't worry. I won't say anything. It's just between us. How's that?'

'All right,' answered Sam.

'Now, how about you doing something for me? How about a little game to cheer me up?'

'OK,' said Sam. 'What do you want to play?'

Then Mike did a strange thing. He took off his shorts and T-shirt and sat down naked on Sam's bed.

'First, take off your shorts. Then I'll show you the rest of the game,' Mike said.

Sam thought it sounded like a stupid idea. So he shook his head.

'What are you afraid of?' teased Mike. 'I'm not going to hurt you.'

'Nothing,' answered Sam. 'I just don't want to, that's all.'

Mike kept talking quietly. 'It's just a game. I'm not going to do anything,' he said.

'Then why should I take my clothes off?'

43

said Sam, who was starting to feel very uncomfortable.

'I just want to look at you. Come on, be a good sport.'

'No,' said Sam. He got off his bed and held on to the top of his shorts.

'Perhaps I'll tell Peter that you missed swimming,' said Mike. 'I bet he's going to be cross with you.'

Sam felt trapped. Why was Mike doing this? He thought Mike was his friend. What kind of a trick was this anyway?

Sam dashed out of the tent and ran into the woods near the swimming pool. He could see Peter and his class practising lifesaving. He saw Mike go over to Peter and tell him something. Sam was scared. What were they saying? He could feel his heart pounding and tears coming into his eyes. He was still crying when Peter finally found him.

'Where have you been? I sent Mike to look for you,' he said.

'He found me,' said Sam, wiping his face and eyes. 'I was just in the tent.'

'What's wrong? What are you crying about?'

Sam didn't know whether to tell Peter what had happened or not. What if he got in trouble for being a bad sport? But, what if Mike tried to trick him like that again? He blurted out the story.

'It's about Mike,' he said. 'He told me to take off all my clothes. He said it was a game. He said I'd get into trouble if I didn't do what he said.'

'Are you sure Mike did that?' Peter asked. Sam nodded.

'Sometimes people do things that are hard to understand,' Peter explained. 'I'll talk to him and straighten this out, Sam.'

Sam was still worried. He told Peter, 'I don't want to get Mike into trouble.'

'Listen, Sam. No one should trick you into playing a game that hurts your feelings. Or a game that you don't like. You did the right thing to tell me. And I don't want you to worry about it. That's my job. To help out.

To solve problems. OK?' said Peter. He put his arm around Sam's shoulders and together they walked towards the swimming pool.

'What's going to happen to Mike?' Sam asked.

'I don't know yet,' answered Peter. 'But that's Mike's problem, not yours. Your problem is catching up on your lifesaving badge. Now jump in.'

Sam felt relieved. He did a racing dive into the pool and swam three lengths as fast as he could.

Maybe his class wouldn't win the Good Sportsmanship Award this year, he thought. It didn't seem so important any more.

Sam still didn't like eating with so many people, or taking showers with them, either. But he did get his lifesaving badge. And most important, Sam found out he could say no and still be a pretty good sport. He thought about going on another school trip next year to practise swerving shots at goal.

Promise Not to Tell

———

Maureen put on her nightdress and got into bed. It was still early, and she liked this time before going to sleep. At least she used to. This was her private time to do whatever she wanted. Tonight she had closed the door and turned on the radio. Now she took out her packet of felt pens to doodle and to write in her diary.

Maureen and her best friend, Beth, kept diaries. Sometimes they'd read pages to each other. Like the time Maureen read the part about when her mum and Pete got married

last year and how she wondered what having a stepfather would be like. Or the time Beth read Maureen the part about her brother getting caught driving a car without a licence. They told each other everything.

Then she heard Pete calling. 'Maureen. Are you ready?' He was going to come up and tuck her in, as he called it. She used to like it when he sat on the bed and talked to her about school and gymnastics. He knew about backward rolls, walkovers, and cartwheels. He had taught her how to play draughts when she had had chicken pox.

But now things were different. He did something he had never done before. He put his hands under the bedclothes and touched her body. He said it was their special secret, and he made her promise never to tell anyone. She had promised.

Tonight when she heard his voice, Maureen scooped up her felt pens and diary and slid them under her pillow. She switched off the light, pulled the bedclothes up over

53

her head, and closed her eyes. She thought, 'I'll pretend I'm asleep. Maybe he'll go away.'

That didn't work. Pete opened the door and said quietly, 'Maureen, I've come to tuck you in. You like that, don't you?'

She lay as still as a stone. She couldn't open her mouth to say a word. She wanted to tell him no . . . please go away.

Pete sat down on the bed and pulled down the bedclothes. He lifted up her nightdress and touched her chest and her tummy and all over. She wanted to yank the bedclothes up under her chin and tell him to go away, to stop it. But she couldn't move. It was like being trapped in a nightmare.

Then Pete smoothed down her nightie, covered her up, and whispered, 'Remember, Maureen, this is our little secret. Promise not to tell Mum or anyone.'

Maureen felt terrible. She was confused and sad at the same time. Why was he doing this? Why was it a secret? she wondered. She needed someone to help her work out what to do. Beth knew everything; maybe she could help.

After school the next day, Beth and Maureen walked through the park and played on the baby swings. They stood on the seats, taking turns twisting the chains into spirals and letting go, twirling and un-twirling.

Maureen flopped down on the grass. 'I'm dizzy,' she said.

Nothing seemed to bother Beth, who rummaged around in her bag for the apple she had saved from lunch. 'Want a bite?'

'Ugh. No,' answered Maureen.

Beth pulled out her diary. 'I've got an entry to read to you.'

Maureen listened as Beth read about a secret club at school. But her mind was on another secret.

'Beth,' Maureen interrupted, 'what would you do if you had a secret that was really awful?'

'Awful? Like what? Read it to me.'

'It's not in my diary. I've never told anyone. I wouldn't dare write it down.'

'Come on, Maureen. I tell you everything,' said Beth.

'This is different. It's about Pete. It's a secret, and anyway, he made me promise not to tell.'

'It's about Pete – your stepfather? What about him?'

'Sometimes when my mum is away, he comes into my room at night. He pretends to tuck me in . . .' Maureen closed her eyes. This was the hard part. 'But he really wants to touch me under my nightdress,' she said.

'You mean all over?' Beth asked.

Maureen looked uneasy. 'Yes. Sometimes he touches me, you know, down there,' she added.

Beth stopped eating. 'That's horrid. What do you do?'

'Nothing,' Maureen answered. 'I don't know what to do.'

'You've got to tell your mum.'

'I can't. I promised Pete I wouldn't. I might get into trouble.'

'Then tell somebody else,' said Beth.

Maureen thought about it for a while. 'What if no one believes me?' she asked.

'You wouldn't lie about a thing like that,' said Beth. 'I'd tell until I found someone who did believe me. That's what I'd do.'

'Like who?' asked Maureen.

'Like Mrs Harvey. Or Miss Taylor, the nurse. Or your aunt. Or my mum. I bet they'd believe you. There are lots of people.'

Maureen began to feel a little better. Beth was the best friend anyone could have, she thought.

'I think I'll talk to Mrs Harvey,' she said.

'Good,' said Beth. 'I'll go with you and wait outside.'

The next day Maureen stayed after school to talk to her form teacher. She told Mrs Harvey that she didn't like being alone with Pete, her stepfather.

'Why not?' asked Mrs Harvey. 'Tell me what the problem is.'

'It's hard to talk about. Pete said it's a secret. He made me promise not to tell anyone,' she said.

'You may feel better if you talk about it,' said Mrs Harvey. 'Some secrets shouldn't be kept.'

'Well,' Maureen said, 'sometimes when we're alone, he touches me in private places. It makes me feel awful.'

Mrs Harvey listened. 'You did the right thing, Maureen. It's good that you told me. Your body belongs to you. No one has the right to touch you that way. It's Pete's secret, not yours.'

'What can I do about it?' asked Maureen.

'You can say, "I don't like it when you touch me like that." But you've already done the most important thing; you've told someone right away. Someone like me who will help you.'

'What can you do?' asked Maureen.

'We can't solve this problem alone,' explained Mrs Harvey. 'There are people who can help, once we tell them what's been happening.'

'Who?' asked Maureen.

'Counsellors and social workers and other people who care for and protect children. They will help make Pete stop it, and help him understand that he is wrong. Your mother can help, too. Things will get better, but it will take time.' Mrs Harvey put her arm around Maureen's shoulders. 'I'm going to help you, and we'll work it out together.'

Beth was waiting for her at the playground, eating an apple. They walked back through the park, to the baby swings, together.

'I'm glad I talked about it,' said Maureen. 'I feel a bit better now.'

Beth smiled. 'Want a bite?' she asked. 'I want to read you my latest entry.'

Maureen took a bite and sat down on one of the little swings to listen.

Some suggestions for where to go for help

National organizations which have local branches — look in your phone directory for the numbers:

NSPCC (National Society for the Prevention of Cruelty to Children)

The Citizens' Advice Bureau: ask for the young people's counsellor

The Town Hall: ask for the duty social worker

The Police: ring your local police station and ask for the youth and community section

The Samaritans

Specialist organizations or individuals who can help:

Family Network c/o the National Children's Home: if you live in the North of England ring 061-236 9873, for the South 0582 422751

Incest Crisis Line: Richard 01-422 5100; Shirley 01-890 4732; Anne 01-302 0570

Incest Survivors' Campaign: for London 01-852 7432 or 01-737 1354; Manchester 061-236 1712; Dundee 0382 21545; Belfast 0232 249 696

Claire Rayner: *Sunday Mirror*, Box 125, London EC1P 1DQ